On the List

Written by Jo Windsor
Illustrated by Richard Hoit

Rigby

Jon and Mary's Wedding Cake

For the Cake Mix
24 eggs
flour
1 packet juice

Cake Icing
6 lemons
powdered sugar

For the Decorations

fish

River Ride Trip

Things I Need to Be Safe
helmet
goggles
flashlight
wetsuit
flippers
life jacket
Other Things
canoe
paddles
clothes (in wet bag)
food
towels

Butterfly Hunting Trip

Things to Take
boxes — big and small,
with holes
butterfly nets
magnifying glass
butterfly book
notebook
pencil
map
tent
sleeping bag
food

Things to Take

big purple pants
white gloves
spotty tie
top hat
ed nose
ig flat shoes
bbits
e with one wheel
orn
bucket

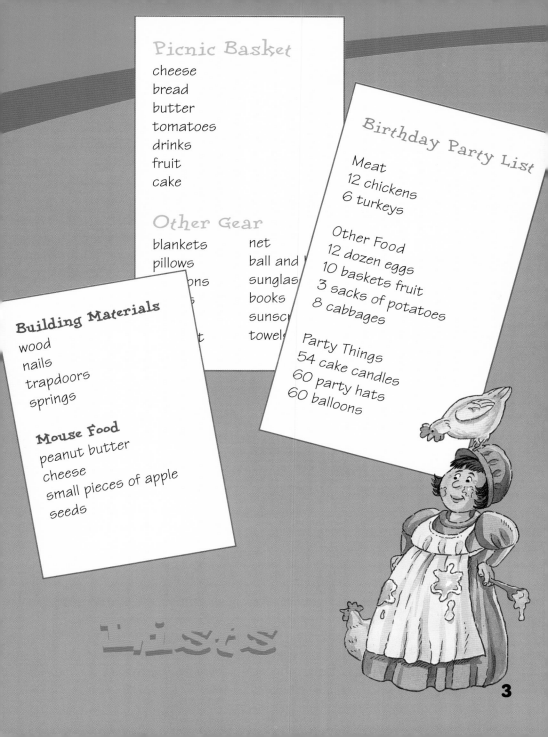

Picnic Basket

cheese
bread
butter
tomatoes
drinks
fruit
cake

Other Gear

blankets
pillows
ons
s

net
ball and
sunglas
books
sunsc
t
towel

Building Materials

wood
nails
trapdoors
springs

Mouse Food

peanut butter
cheese
small pieces of apple
seeds

Birthday Party List

Meat
12 chickens
6 turkeys

Other Food
12 dozen eggs
10 baskets fruit
3 sacks of potatoes
8 cabbages

Party Things
54 cake candles
60 party hats
60 balloons

Lists

3

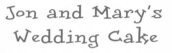

Hello, I'm Wally.
I make the biggest and best cakes in town. I make birthday cakes, party cakes, and wedding cakes. The next cake I have to make is a big wedding cake for Jon and Mary Smith. They are having 300 people at their wedding. When I have a big cake to do, I make a list.

Jon and Mary's Wedding Cake

For the Cake Mix
24 eggs
flour
1 packet juice

Cake Icing
6 lemons
powdered sugar

For the Decorations
jelly beans
chocolate fish
silver balls
nuts
ribbon

4

Hello, I'm Sue.
I'm a River Rider. I love riding the rivers. The rivers I ride can be dangerous. When you ride rivers, you need special gear. Here is a list of the things I take.

River Ride Trip

Things I Need to Be Safe
helmet
goggles
flashlight
wetsuit
flippers
life jacket
Other Things
canoe
paddles
clothes (in wet bag)
food
towels

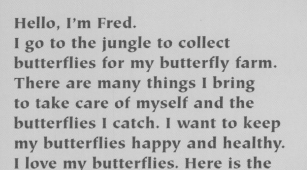

Hello, I'm Fred.
I go to the jungle to collect butterflies for my butterfly farm. There are many things I bring to take care of myself and the butterflies I catch. I want to keep my butterflies happy and healthy. I love my butterflies. Here is the list of the things I take on my butterfly hunt.

Butterfly Hunting Trip

Things to Take
boxes – big and small, with holes
butterfly nets
magnifying glass
butterfly book
notebook
pencil
map
tent
sleeping bag
food

Hello, I'm Cook.
The king is having a
birthday party. It is a very
busy time for me. I have to
get up early and visit the
market to get things for the
birthday party. Here is my
shopping list.

Birthday Party List

Meat
12 chickens
6 turkeys

Other Food
12 dozen eggs
10 baskets fruit
3 sacks of potatoes
8 cabbages

Party Things
54 cake candles
60 party hats
60 balloons

10

Hello, I'm Clown.
I go to lots of birthday parties.
I make the kids laugh. I have
to make sure I take all the
things I need for my tricks.
I make a list so that I don't
forget anything!

Things to Take

big purple pants
white gloves
spotty tie
top hat
red nose
big flat shoes
rabbits
bike with one wheel
horn
bucket

Hello, I'm Mr. Green.
I have a big family that loves
to go to the lake. The kids like
to swim, fish, and play ball. Mrs.
Green likes to read, and I like to
sleep. Before we go, I make a list
of all the things we need to take.

Picnic Basket

cheese
bread
butter
tomatoes
drinks
fruit
cake

Other Gear

blankets	net
pillows	ball and bat
cushions	sunglasses
games	books
hats	sunscreen
fly swatter	towels

Hello, I'm Fran.
I sell mouse traps. My traps
are very good for catching mice.
I make traps of all different
shapes and sizes. The mice
I catch go to good homes.
When I build a trap, I make
a list of the things I need.

Building Materials
wood
nails
trapdoors
springs

Mouse Food
peanut butter
cheese
small pieces of apple
seeds

Lists

You can write lists for:

What to take
Where to go
What to wear
What to buy
What you need
What to do

How to write a list:

Step One
Think about:

- Why am I writing this list
- What is the list for
- What things do I want on my list

Step Two
Write down the things you want on your list.

(You could write headings
for your list to sort the things
into groups.)

Step Three
Check your list:

- **Have you forgotten
  anything?**
- **Is there anything you can
  take off your list?**

Remember
**You can use your list as a
checklist. You can check
off the things you have
or have done.**

Shopping List for
Mom's Party

Food
cake
strawberries
cherries
chocolate

Decorations for Cake
candles
silver beads
ribbons

Fun things
party hats
balloons

▬▬ Guide Notes

Title: On the List
Stage: Fluency (2)

Text Form: Lists
Approach: Guided Reading
Processes: Thinking Critically, Exploring Language, Processing Information
Written and Visual Focus: List, Speech Bubbles

THINKING CRITICALLY
(sample questions)
- Where would Wally go to get the things that he has written on his list?
- Why do you think Fran included food on her list?
- Why do you think Fred included a map on his list?
- What do you think would happen if Cook forgot to put the candles on her list? What would the king say?

EXPLORING LANGUAGE

Terminology
Spread, author and illustrator credits, ISBN number

Vocabulary
Clarify: silver, collect, magnifying glass, market, cushions, springs, fly swatter, gear
Nouns: cake, river, map, list
Verbs: ride, hunt, fish
Singular/plural: mouse/mice, butterfly/butterflies, egg/eggs, canoe/canoes

Print Conventions
Colon, dash (boxes – big and small)
Apostrophes – possessive (Mary's wedding cake), contraction (I'm, don't)
Parenthesis: (in wet bag)

Phonological Patterns
Focus on short and long vowel **i** (l**i**st, f**i**sh, tr**i**p, t**i**me, t**i**e, m**i**ce)
Discuss root words – biggest, parties, dangerous, butterflies
Look at suffix **ous** (danger**ous**)